PASS IT
FORWARD

PASS IT
FORWARD

PATRICK JONES

MINNEAPOLIS

Darby Creek
A division of Lerner Publishing Group, Inc.
241 First Avenue North
Minneapolis, MN 55401 USA

For reading levels and more information, look up this title at www.lernerbooks.com.

Front cover: © Albo/Shutterstock.com

Main body text set in Janson Text LT Std 12/17.5.
Typeface provided by Adobe Systems.

Library of Congress Cataloging-in-Publication Data

The Cataloging-in-Publication Data for *Pass It Forward* is on file at the Library of Congress.
ISBN 978-1-5124-1125-6 (lib. bdg.)
ISBN 978-1-5124-1209-3 (pbk.)
ISBN 978-1-5124-1136-2 (EB pdf)

Manufactured in the United States of America
1-39640-21283-4/6/2016

To Anna, Jenny, and Julie

WEDNESDAY MORNING
FEBRUARY 8
Lucas Washington's apartment

Mom's alarm blares from her room. In our tiny one-bedroom, the buzz wakes me up too.

I roll over on the rough, worn sofa where I sleep. I lift my old watch off the orange crate that serves as a table. It is 5:00 a.m. Mom needs to be at her hospital job by 7:00. About when she starts lifting patients from their wheelchairs, I'll be elevating iron at the school weight room.

I pull the thin blanket over me and shiver in

our heatless apartment. A few times this winter when it got really cold, Mom would leave open the oven after she'd cooked some packaged food left over from her other job at the nursing home. It is only once a month they clean the pantry. Mostly we live on Hamburger Helper without the hamburger.

"Mom, you okay?" I yell. It seems all I ever do anymore is yell. I can't seem to control the sound of my voice. Over the summer, before my senior year, my voice got even deeper and I had a late-life growth spurt. I went from a small point guard to a passing forward, but Coach switched me again halfway through the season. As soon as I got the ball to shoot, we got hot— unlike this apartment—and qualified for the state finals, which start tonight. Since our record is the worst of any team in Alabama's 6A conference, we won't play any of our tournament games in our own gym. Coach says we all need to kick in for gas money. If we make it to the semi-finals, the games will be at the Birmingham Convention Complex.

"Luke, come help me!" Mom shouts from the other room. I get up, rub the sleep out of my eyes, and walk through our mostly bare apartment. There is no sense having stuff if one day you might come home to find it all on the curb or in a Dumpster. I figure if I don't have anything, I can't lose anything or have somebody take it away again. "Hurry up, Luke!"

I use my new long legs to get to her room in sprinter's time. I gained all this size but didn't lose my speed. I'm awkward everyplace except on the basketball court. I help Mom out of bed just like she'll help others later today. It seems like heavy lifting is all our family does.

For us, nothing comes easy. Easy comes with a price that we can't afford.

WEDNESDAY AFTERNOON
FEBRUARY 8
Jackson High School

The first bell rings to start class, but I don't
move a hard muscle. I sit motionless in the
high school counselor's office. "You have a
better chance of winning the lottery than
getting drafted to play in the NBA—or
even getting recruited to play D-1 college
ball," Mr. Edwards tells me during our first-
ever meeting. Coach had said I should meet
with Mr. Edwards because colleges might

want to talk to me after we win State.

"Every corner store in my neighborhood sells tickets; maybe I'll buy one," I joke. His brown tie is tied so tightly around his neck, it looks like his face should be turning purple.

"What should I do?"

Edwards's expression flashes a "stop bothering me" look. "Maybe a trade school?"

"I don't know anybody going to trade school." Actually, I don't know anyone going to college, period. My oldest brother, Mark, went off to college to play ball, but he broke his ankle, lost his scholarship, and put his college career in the rearview.

"Russell Walker is going to A+ Auto Mechanics this summer. You should talk to him."

"I don't know him. Anyway, I got basketball camp in the summer. If I'm gonna make the—"

"Lucas, just because you got big doesn't mean you should dream so big. Find Russell."

That will be easy. When you go to a school where half the students drop out before graduation, the class sizes get smaller.

You can get to know the few who remain.

The second bell rings for class to start. I take my time. I'd rather be late than walk in the hall at its busiest time, wearing ill-fitting clothes from the church's clothing drive. Fewer people seeing me means fewer can laugh at me. Not that most people peer up from their phones. Everybody walks head down, making senseless noise, trudging from class to class, trying to get smart enough to get out of here. This place is like that TV show *The Walking Dead* that some people talk about.

I'm lost in thought. I bump into this fat kid who has never missed a meal. I apologize, but instead of saying "It's all right," he says through laughter, "How is the weather up there, freak?"

My mind flashes back to Edwards's insult. I fill my mouth with spit and let it drop on him. "Raining."

WEDNESDAY EVENING
FEBRUARY 8
On the bus to Austin, Alabama
Game 1

There's a loud thud when my head hits the
top of the bus. I think the bus driver found
every pothole in the ninety miles north from
Birmingham to Austin. When it happens as
we pull into the parking lot, Nate laughs. Nate
wants my dignity because I took his power-
forward minutes.

"What's so funny?" I ask. He sits across

from me. Our new coach doesn't assign seats like our last coach, Coach T, who got ousted when we had a losing record last year. Everybody does what they want, kind of like on the court. Our game is playground ball at the high school level, which works for me since my job is to shoot and rebound.

"You. Everything about you." Like the fat kid in the hall, Nate can't stop laughing at me.

I put my history textbook in my bag. I studied during the ride, while most of the other guys scrolled through their phones. Part of me wants to spit on Nate too, but I can't treat a teammate like that. I try to ignore him, but he won't let up.

"That's enough, Nate," Coach Unser says. Nate grumbles like he has rocks in his mouth.

"Maybe if you were more serious, you'd get more playing time," Coach lectures Nate.

"I had playing time, but you gave it to that gangly giraffe." Nate makes animal sounds.

"That *athlete* scores points, brings down rebounds, and crashes the net. And for a forward, he has the vision of a point guard. You do any of those things as good as Lucas, then you'll play."

Nate grumbles again before exiting the bus. "Thanks for saying that, Coach," I say.

"It's all true. I wish I'd seen it earlier. I don't know why Coach T didn't start you."

"Elijah and David are great guards and I'm too small for center. Paul's an oak," I say.

"You see the game like a guard, so you make great passes. That gets you open to get better shots. You give, so you get the ball back to put in the net. That's basketball, that's life."

"You sound like the minister at my grandmother's church," I joke. Coach doesn't laugh.

"Basketball *is* life, Lucas. Follow the rules and play the game right, and you'll win." I nod in agreement, even though everything he just said about life is wrong. Just ask my brother Mark.

SATURDAY MORNING
FEBRUARY 11
On the bus to Gardendale

I hear the booming bass through the closed window of the limo. It is 5:15 in the morning. I just started my two-hour bus ride to a mall that is fifteen minutes away by car. By limo, I bet it is even faster. People in limos are rich, and the rich don't have to obey rules. Ask Mark about that too.

I turn up the volume on my busted CD player. A rubber band holds it together so it can play. I listen to a CD of beach white noise I got from the public library. The waves calm me. I have never seen or been on a real ocean beach, but it seems peaceful. Unlike this bus, unlike that limo. Since so much of the rest of my life is noisy, especially our new apartment, the bus is my quiet time.

Still, I wish I had a job closer to home, but there are no jobs for adults, let alone high school kids. Like Mom, I haul my tired self on a city bus for the long ride. Mom and me have another thing in common: she lifts people at work, while last night I lifted my team to victory. We blew out Austin. I topped the team in points, boards, and blocked shots. By the third quarter I felt sorry for Austin. We're the Jackson Mustangs, but I bet the Austin Black Bears felt like Daniel thrown into the lions' den.

I'm enjoying the waves when I feel a tap on my knee. It is Trina Saunders, a girl who lives in an apartment across the way. She's in history with me and plays on the girls' basketball team.

"Hey, Lucas, congratulations on last night," she says and then goes all wide-smile.

"Thanks," I mumble into my left hand. I always try to hide my mouth full of crooked teeth from girls.

"Where are you going this early in the morning?" she asks brightly. How can she be so giddy at this hour?

"Work."

"Me too," she says. She tells me about her new job at Wal-Mart. "I don't mind the commute. The bus ride gives me time to read." She flashes a big book at me.

My grandmother would smile if she saw this. The book Trina shows me is the Bible.

SATURDAY AFTERNOON
FEBRUARY 11
Lucas Washington's apartment

The squealing of tires announces Mark's arrival. I sigh when I see his green Mustang out our apartment window. I had used a phone at work to ask him to meet me there. He never showed at Ryan's, but instead he came here. That's not good.

The two locks on the door fail in their mission to keep out criminals. Mark unlocks the knob and dead bolt and walks inside.

He wears a Memphis Grizzlies jersey with Zach Randolph's name on the back. Mark owns one for every player. As soon as the Grizzlies get a new player, he buys a new jersey. He gave me one once for my birthday, but Mom made me give it back. He's not even supposed to set foot in our apartment.

"How much you want?" He reaches into his pocket and takes out a big stack of bills.

"Fifty." The little cash I make helps Mom with the rent. Mark peels off a hundred for me.

"What for?" Mark inspects the apartment. He could stand in the middle, pivot like the center he used to be, and almost touch each wall. "It doesn't have to be a handout. If you want to—"

I cut him off before he can say "work for me." "I met this girl," I say quickly. "I need new clothes."

Mark says nothing. He opens the cupboards in the kitchen and examines the emptiness. Next, he picks through the cluttered counter. It is covered with bills. Unpaid, I assume.

"Give this to Mom." He offers me another hundred. "I know she won't take it from me."

I'm reaching to take the fresh bill when I hear the doorknob start to turn. Mom is home early from work. She yells first at me for letting Mark in. Then she turns to Mark and tells him to get out, shouting, "You will not soil my home!"

"Some home," Mark jokes. Mom rushes forward and slaps his face like he was ten again.

"You got a stack of bills." He points to the counter, and then to his full hand. "And so do I. Let me help, Mom."

"Mark, why—" I start, but stop when Mom grabs Mark's arm and pulls at it. He doesn't resist, but Mom slips and falls down on the gray carpet. Mark reaches down to help her up.

"Out of my house!" is Mom's answer

to his offer of help. Mark throws a hundred at her and leaves. Mom takes the crisp green paper in her heavily callused hands and rips it in half.

SATURDAY EVENING FEBRUARY 11
Cullman High School gym
Game 2

The roar of the Cullman High crowd doesn't bother me at all. That hardly anybody from Jackson is making the trip to see us play bothers me. Of the few who did, Trina is not one of them. That bothers me too. But Mom hurting her back again is what bothers me most. I'm off my game.

"You need a rest?" Coach asks before we

start the second half. We're only up by ten.

"No, I need to play better," I huff. "That's what I need to do."

"Then do it!" Coach pats my back while his words and glare kick my butt into gear. It's hard to get motivated when playing against a bad team. Even in playground ball, I always played older kids. Mark taught me that only iron sharpens iron. He taught me lots of things. Now he wants to teach me new things. No, thanks.

"Lucas, you need to focus tonight more than ever," Coach says, almost in a whisper. I lean closer like he's telling me a secret. "Up in the stands is an old college buddy of mine. He's a recruiter for a certain college in Southern California. Would you like to meet him sometime?"

"Yes, sir," I mumble as the buzzer sounds to start the second half.

"Get loud, Lucas, get noticed!" Coach yells. I run onto the court. I set myself by the Cullman guy next to me. He's taller, but I'm more muscular. When the ball comes to him, he tries to drive, but I get into position. He charges into the human roadblock I'll be for the rest of this game.

Elijah turns the ball over. The Cullman guard shoots a rock and I crash the net. I grab the rebound and see David breaking. I make a long pass. He dribbles, cuts, and passes to Elijah trailing behind. Elijah looks to shoot, but he's covered. I pass and set the pick, and he rolls—the shot is his. It smacks off the backboard and I follow to bang bodies underneath. The ball comes into my hands, and I slam it through the net.

The hometown crowd boos as we celebrate. Cullman brings the ball up. Their game is too slow, their leaps too short, and their muscles too small. And after that last play, they know it. I gaze up into the stands for Coach's friend and think to myself, *I've always wanted to see California.*

SUNDAY MORNING
FEBRUARY 12
Ryan's Steak Buffet

The silver plastic busing tray thumps when
I drop it onto the metal counter. There are
two things louder in the kitchen. One is the
grumbling of my empty stomach—the stale
Pop-Tarts I ate for breakfast on the bus are
hungry for company. The other is the clock
on the wall that clicks more slowly the closer it
gets to my break. I can do heavy buffet damage
in my fifteen minutes.

"Did your team win last night?" Mr. Robbins, one of the assistant managers, asks. He's got a big gut and thin gray hair, and wears the same ugly maroon polo shirt as me, except mine fits.

I tell him about the game. He pretends to be interested, a lot like Trina this morning on the bus. I guess she'd rather be reading her Bible than talking to somebody like me. Or maybe she's just making up her mind about me, wondering if I'm worth her precious time.

"Mr. Robbins, sir, do you think when the season is over I could get more hours?"

He pulls on his tight shirt. "You work as many hours on weekends as we can allow you to work for the week."

"After the season, I could work after school."

He frowns, like always. If I were fifty and working a job like this, I'd never smile either. "It already takes you two hours to get here. How would that work with your school schedule?"

I want to tell him that if I don't get a college scholarship by the end of basketball season, I will probably quit school without graduating and go to work full-time. Mom didn't like it when my older brother Josh dropped out, but I don't see any choice. Her back hurts too bad for her to work. No work, no money. It is all on me. "I'll figure it out."

"I don't see it." He walks away, and I pull garbage from the bus cart. Our customers waste more food in one meal than I have in my whole life. I've always been hungry, *always*. The only decent meals I ever got were at school, until I started working here. Like I told Trina this morning when I told her that I worked at Ryan's, the food here's not good, but there's a lot of it.

As soon as the clock strikes ten, I race to the cashier. I give her my money. She rings up the price with my discount. I have fifteen minutes to inhale food like we inhaled Cullman last night.

SUNDAY AFTERNOON
FEBRUARY 12
Grandma Washington's house

"Amen," my grandmother says. Mom just
winces. Her back is killing her, but she still
managed to go with her mom to church.
They've talked about nothing but church since
dinner started.

"Minister Oster was right," Grandmother
says as we eat greasy Chinese takeout.
"Remember Proverbs 3:9–10: 'Honor the Lord
with your wealth, with the firstfruits of all

your crops; then your barns will be filled to overflowing, and your vats will brim over with new wine.' "

Mom doesn't agree loud or long enough, so she gets a glare from Grandma. Normally that's the way Grandma stares at me. She doesn't like that I work instead of attending church.

"I heard from Rachel last night." Grandma starts bragging on her youngest daughter's children. "Both their sororities are doing food drives for the poor, as the Lord would want."

Whenever Grandma mentions Mom's sister Rachel, her husband, or her kids, Mom's face reacts in pain like Grandma is pouring small white salt crystals into big open wounds.

"What will you do after graduation?" Grandma clicks her green-painted nails on the table.

"After our game last night," I say, all excited, "I think I'll be the first high school player from Alabama to succeed going straight from high school to the pros."

Grandma points at Mom and shakes her head. "Your children and their foolish schemes."

When I make it, I'll be the only of Mom's three sons to succeed. That's a poor shooting percentage. "Mark is a criminal," Grandma says, full of fury. "And Josh failed at even doing that."

Mom winces in pain. Her hurt back isn't up to the lashes from Grandma's whip-like tongue.

"Don't worry, Mom," I say. "I'm gonna make it somehow. Just have some faith in me."

Mom smiles, but Grandma clicks her nails harder on the table. "Fool-headed big dreams."

I stand. That gets Grandma's attention and the clicking stops. "How come you believe in Jesus, who you've never met, but you can't have even a little faith in your own flesh and blood?"

SUNDAY EVENING FEBRUARY 12
Tuxedo Park

The ball whooshing through the net contrasts with the blaring sirens in the distance. "Li'l Mark, that was a cold shot!" Kevin shouts to me from across the dimly-lit court. I don't disagree or tell him how I hate that he and all of Mark's old friends I play against use that name. I'm big now. And I'm not Mark.

Kevin likes the shot even more because

it wins us the game. Kevin, Tony, and Scott decide to take a break before we go again. Scott's new to our Sunday night game. He replaced my brother Josh.

Even though it's cold outside, Mark's friends cool off more by drinking forty-ounce beers.

"How'd you get so good?" Scott asks as he offers me a forty. I decline.

"Playing them." I point at Kevin and Tony. They laugh, but I'm not sure why. If they would have stayed in school and kept up their grades, they would have been scholarship material. While a college coach would've smoothed out their moves, their instincts for the game—like Mark's— were so good, they could have made the NBA. Instead, they get a game at tiny Tuxedo Park.

"Does Mark even play anymore?" Scott asks.

"Not since he broke his ankle," I answer, which for some reason makes Kevin smirk.

"Mark's too busy with other things," Kevin says. Kevin and Tony laugh. They're not only Mark's friends. They're also part of his crew. They traded hitting jumpers for likely wearing County Jail jumpsuits. Me, I just want to wear a basketball uniform as long as I can, but that's easier said than done. The court comes easy, yet my shot at making it is slim; the streets are hard but the payoff's every day. Lots of risk, but lots of rewards. Mark showed me that too.

They finish their beers and we hit the court again. When Kevin makes a crazy dunk, I tease him, saying, "Great shot, Kobe." He cracks up every time I say that. When Mark first introduced me to the park and the game, people got nicknamed according to the player they most resembled, which was normally an NBA star. Kevin would see a Kobe move on Friday, try it out on Saturday, and by Sunday have it down stone cold. I was the same, except I didn't see the moves on TV. I saw them on the court made by my oldest brother. As much as I don't like it, I know I'll always be "Li'l Mark."

We play until my curfew. Then I go home to study. They head off in another direction.

MONDAY MORNING
FEBRUARY 13
Jackson High School

There's crackle but no snap or pop from the rip-off Rice Krispies served in the cafeteria. I crack that to the guys on the team, who sit together every morning. Everybody laughs except Nate. Instead, he'd rather laugh at me. "Luke, you don't need a spoon; you need a big shovel."

Elijah cracks up at Nate putting me down. I answer by eating even faster. My guess is Nate had something other than macaroni with butter for dinner, but that's all I know how to cook. Mom stayed in bed last night. She even called in sick to both her jobs, which she never does. Working these hard jobs, Mom's hurt her hands, arms, legs, and feet at one time or another. Like some wounded soldier, she usually keeps pressing on, but not today. That's how I know it's bad.

Pretty soon everybody's laughing at everything. It's the sound of a winning team. That's on me. I started the season as back-up guard, and now I'm the lead scoring forward. In our first season game, I got zero minutes. In our last playoff game, I had a triple-double. Things change.

Nate makes another crack. "Luke, your stomach's a vacuum sucking down every—"

"Yeah, I'm a vacuum," I say, interrupting his insult. "A vacuum that sucks down rebounds."

"And smacks down shots," Elijah adds.

He's our captain, our leader. Elijah's okay.
The thing about following leaders, though,
is they can create a vacuum in their wake.
Josh followed, and I saw where he ended up
going. Down. The streets are a vacuum of
their own.

I know why Nate's upset—I took his
minutes—but I don't get why he can't let it
go. I shrug and slurp down the last of the
milk and cereal as the bell rings for class.
Since first period equals Mrs. Thompson's
class, I don't want to be late. Something
about her makes me not want to disappoint
her by doing anything wrong. Kind of like
with Mom.

The only thing louder than the bell is
the noise of a hundred free-breakfast kids
nourished, like me, probably for the first
time in hours, burning it off and heading
to class. Normally I hate the noise of the
crowded hallways and would put on my
beach CD, but I welcome the clatter this
morning. At home, ever since she caught
Mark in our apartment, silence is all I get

from Mom. That is, unless you count the groans of her pain. It's not my fault, but she's acting like she blames me for letting Mark in the door that day. That's a burden too large even for my broad shoulders.

MONDAY AFTERNOON
FEBRUARY 13
Jackson High School gym

Coach's whistle screams like Mom's old teapot.
Both mean hot water.

"Elijah, you need to move the ball
quicker," Coach says. "And, Lucas, you need
to fight harder to get free." I want to say
"That's what I've been doing all my life," but
I say nothing.

The thing about Coach Unser is that he
teaches us plays, but in games, he doesn't get

mad if we freelance. As long as we knock down
two or three, he's fine. It's an easy system.

Mark played college ball in Tennessee.
That is a basketball state, unlike Alabama.
People here think basketball is something tall
people do to fill time between football and
baseball. Mark complained about his coach's
system limiting his freedom to play his game.
Mark even blamed his coach for the broken
ankle that finished his college career. The
ankle never healed right, but I wonder if that's
all that stops Mark from still getting a game.
He doesn't want to remember or talk about it.

"Luke, wake up!" Elijah throws the ball
at me. I catch it, take a step. Head fake even
though nobody's in front of me. I do it like I
learned it. Not from Coach, but from Mark.
Ball goes in. Three.

Coach tells us to start practice. I square
off against Nate. He plays hard and smart and
strong. Trouble is that I'm harder, smarter,
and stronger than him. I grew up and got buff.
He didn't.

I don't just shut Nate down—I give him

a spanking worse than his mom ever did. If there were a score sheet for scrimmage, he'd be nothing but negatives: turnovers, fouls, and missed shots. The one time he almost beat me, I hustled back and rejected his shot with harsh intent.

After wind sprints to end practice, Nate comes over to me. He breathes heavy. "Man, Luke, how come you had to grow four inches and put on twenty pounds of muscle over one summer? These were supposed to be my minutes. My tournament. My scholarship opportunity."

He wants an apology he won't get. "I guess wrong place, wrong time for me," Nate says.

In front of me is Nate, but in my ear, I hear Josh saying those same words over and over.

MONDAY EVENING
FEBRUARY 13
Lucas Washington's apartment

"You are late." Mom's three words of disapproval deafen me. At least she's talking to me again, but when she does, it's all anger and pain.

"I'm sorry," I mutter. After practice, I still wanted a game. Nobody was playing at Tuxedo, so I caught the bus to the UAB. There I got a game against college players. I lost, but I'll call it a win since I didn't let myself get down getting beat by guys older and better than me.

"You need to sit down and study." Mom points at the empty chair.

"Way I remember it, Mark never studied and he still went to college. So I don't—"

"For less than one year." Mom slaps my face with her words. I join Mom at the kitchen table, where she's eating Dollar Store popcorn. It doesn't pop, just like the cafeteria breakfast cereal. It seems nothing around here lives up to the hype. Not cereal, not snacks. Not Mark, maybe not me.

"Stuff happens," I say. Mom's hard look somehow grows harder. "It wasn't his—"

"Luke, don't you have studying to do?" Mom camouflages her command as a query.

I think about Mark. He was twice as good as me on the court. Now, he won't even play. He's too busy making green to bother with the orange ball. "Why didn't you take Mark's money—at least just until you can go back to work?" The question attacks her ears, but it is her back that Mom clutches like I'd stabbed her.

"I don't want his dirty money in my house," Mom says. I look around the small, empty apartment. This isn't a house or a home. It is shelter from the storm of our endless poverty.

"But—" I get in one word before Mom blocks my sentence with a "shut-up" stare. The only things hotter than Mom's angry eyes are Mark's hundreds burning like hellfire in my pockets.

The more Mom talks, the worse I feel. She's trying to inspire me to be better than Mark and Josh, but her words drag me down like a weight. "My back is killing me," Mom moans.

"It will get better," I say, not sure if I believe it, but I know I have to stay positive—always.

WEDNESDAY MORNING
FEBRUARY 15
Jackson High School playground

The heavy weights clank as I push them up
and down across my chest. They echo in
the silence. Like most mornings, it is just
me in the school's old weight room. There's
no carpet on the cold floor, and the old
equipment lingers with the odor of ancient
sweat. I towel off and head toward the
playground to catch a quick pick-up game in
the half hour before school starts.

"Hey, Lucas." It's Trina Saunders. I say something back, but I doubt she hears it through those giant red headphones covering her ears. "You got another game tonight?"

I motion to the headphones. She removes them. "Yes." I can't look her in the eye. "When we win, then we go to the semi-finals, but not 'til the twenty-fourth."

"So no game this coming Saturday?" she asks.

I shake my head no. She smiles pretty but says nothing. Saturday night is my lame school's late Valentine's Day dance. Maybe she wants me to ask her but wonders if I can afford it. I survey the schoolyard. Lots of other folks wear big headphones like Trina, but they also dress nice, got fancy phones, and act like they got money. I bet they do. I know a lot of them didn't earn it working a crappy job a long bus ride away, like us. They earned it standing on a corner.

"I hope you win."

"You don't need hope when you're as good as us." She laughs as pretty as she smiles.

I feel the empty space in my pocket where

one of Mark's hundreds once was. I gave it to Mom but told her it was from work. She didn't question it. She used it to help pay the rent, I hope.

Trina stares down at the pavement below. "There's a school dance on Saturday night."

It feels like I'm still sweating from the weight room. "I know."

Then we fall silent as everyone rushes around us, their loud voices filling the air. It seems like people try to get all their yelling and laughing out before they go inside, except it doesn't work. "I probably have to work anyway," Trina finally says. She turns her back and walks away. I don't say anything.

WEDNESDAY AFTERNOON FEBRUARY 15
Jackson High School

The Bunsen burner whooshes in the science lab when I turn it on. Elijah is my lab partner. He's as jokey off the court as he is serious on it. Mrs. Thompson tells him to knock it off. And he does. She's always calling him out. She never notices me, as if I'm invisible. Fine with me.

"So I was going to ask Trina to the dance," I whisper. "But . . ."

"She has a fine one of those for sure." I bite my lip so I don't laugh. "So why not?"

Elijah's a great point guard who feeds me the ball when and where I want it. I guess I owe him the truth. Or half of it. "It's about money." He nods. He knows this life too.

The other half of the truth is, as much as I'd like to go out with Trina, I also know Mom had two kids before she was eighteen, just like her mother. More mouths, less money. I know things happen that can make things get real fast, and I refuse to follow in those footsteps.

I turn my attention to the experiment, concentrating hard since Elijah's acting goofy.

"That's a good job, Lucas," Mrs. Thompson says. Elijah giggles. Why is she busting me?

She notices the embarrassed expression on my face. "No, Lucas, I'm serious. Excellent!"

This is the first time I can remember any teacher, except a coach or P.E. guy, telling me I was doing something right. "Could you explain to the class what you are doing, Lucas?"

I stand up, and everybody else is sitting so I feel like a hulking monster. I start to explain, but I stumble over my words. I hate talking in front of the class. I'm relieved when Elijah takes over for the save.

After he's done, Mrs. Thompson says, "Well, thank you, Elijah. Perhaps when Lucas becomes a scientist or doctor, you could be his spokesperson." Everybody cracks up at that.

I stare into the blue flame like it was a crystal ball. If I don't make the NBA, I could go to college and study for one of those jobs— except for one thing. College costs money. Maybe that's why money is green. It means "go." If you haven't got it, you're stuck.

WEDNESDAY EVENING
FEBRUARY 15
Lee High School gym
Game 3

The swoosh of the ball through the net sounds
like the collective sigh from the hometown Lee
crowd when I sink two more free throws. I've
got almost as many points from the line as from
the lanes. They've double-teamed me all night,
trying to stop another double-double. Instead the
Lee hacks have fouled me or left another Mustang
free to shoot, mostly Paul tossing up hooks.

"Nice job!" Jeremy says to Paul with a wide smile. Paul earned it, passing the ball with speed and vision. Even though there's only a minute left, Coach leaves in the starters. Not to pile up the score, although we're doing that, but because Coach knows recruiters attend tournament games.

Lee inbounds, but their point guard plays sloppy and Elijah steals the ball. Rather than racing for the basket, he slows up and surveys the court. I race toward the baseline and break my double-team. I flip my thumb in the air, calling the play that I saw Mark do a hundred times.

Elijah nods and dribbles, almost acting bored. He sets to shoot. I drive toward the basket. Elijah hurls the ball high toward the net—not a shot, but a pass. In one motion, I snatch the ball and stuff it in the basket. I pretend I can hear recruiters scribbling my name in their notebooks.

I would've thought that since we're in Huntsville, home of rocket scientists and their offspring, their team would play a smart game. School smarts doesn't always equal court intelligence. The only way I will get a scholarship is through basketball, but only to a school that doesn't have high academic standards.

After the alley-oop, Coach pulls me. "Great game, Lucas, but that's enough for tonight. We've got to save some for the semi-finals." I get a pat on my sweaty back from Coach.

"I don't know how to save anything," I say as I grab some pine.

Truth is, I have saved one thing. I've saved myself from walking in both of my brothers' footsteps, even if I do wear Mark's hand-me-down Chuck knock-offs. Mark only wears Versace now. But even my cheap sneaks are better than whatever footwear County makes Josh wear.

SATURDAY MORNING
FEBRUARY 18
Ryan's Steak Buffet

Mark's laughter booms over the din of late-morning diners at Ryan's. When I hear Mark from a few tables away, I duck behind a table like I'm picking something off the floor, hoping he doesn't see me.

"Can I get some shrimp or what?" Mark yells out. It is ten o'clock in the morning. Mr. Robbins furls his thin brow and waddles his fat body in Mark's direction. He'll need reinforcements. It is not just Mark, but also Tony, Scott, Kevin, and four girls I don't know.

The laughter ends and I hear, even from my long distance, some harsh words exchanged, many only four letters. "My little brother works here!" Mark shouts. "Let me talk to him."

Rather than having Mr. Robbins find me, I stand up as straight as I can and walk over to Mark. He and his friends laugh when they see me. Maybe if I were in their dancing-all-night party shoes, I'd laugh at the sight of me as well. "Mark, we don't put out shrimp until lunch."

"What time is it?" The question cracks up his entourage. From the crazed sound of their chortles, they are no doubt in need of food to soak up whatever chemicals they've ingested.

I look at my watch. He pulls out his phone. It shines.

"What, don't you have a phone?"

He knows why. "Or some decent clothes? You buy some clothes with that cash?" I shake my head, embarrassed at the scene we're making. Mr. Robbins has retreated to the other side of the room. "Luke, you don't have to be doing this crap. You're my little brother—I'll teach you what you need to know. We could hang out all the time if you work with me—"

I feel a twinge when he says "little brother." All I ever wanted, growing up, was to be like Mark. But I shake my head, enough to almost knock off the hairnet they make us wear.

Then I change the subject. "We're going to be in the semi-finals. The game is Friday."

"Busy." Mark sits down, pulls in his chair, and pretends I don't exist.

One word is all my brother has for me. I get it. He can't stand basketball ever since he broke his ankle and lost his dreams. I head back to work. Mark turns to his friends. We don't talk again until just before he exits. He hands me a tip. It is another crisp hundred. I pocket it.

SATURDAY AFTERNOON FEBRUARY 18
Jefferson County Jail

One kid's crying is so piercing that it injures
my ears. There's nothing I can do about
it. I'm still stuck in the lobby at Jefferson
County Jail with Mom. As fast as I move on
the court is as slow as I move in this long line.
I study the other visitors and realize I know a
lot of them.

The jail, unlike Holman State Prison where
Josh last did time, only allows visiting one day

of the week. For one hour. Two people at a time. One pane of glass. Two phones.

"Hey, Luke, how're you doing?" Josh asks when he picks up the phone. "How's basketball season coming along?"

I tell him about the state tournament. He wants all the details because inside, there's no news. It is like he lives on Mars, until Mom and I or his wife and four kids visit.

"You play hard and you'll get yourself a college scholarship like Mark. But unlike him, maybe you won't blow it." The bitterness in Josh's voice feels like sandpaper on my skin.

"I'll try to do my best," I say, trying to stay humble. "The next team we play is—"

"Listen, little brother, you don't *try* anything. You *do*. You're it." He points at Mom. "You're Mom's last chance out of crummy apartments and off of government handouts."

Mom looks as if she's embarrassed for herself and proud of me at the same time.

"You can make some real money," Josh says. "Not what you can make on the corner or even in a corner office, but NBA money.

Buy her a house, a car, all the things I never could do."

I try talking about something else, but like on the court, Josh stands his ground. He never was as good of a player as Mark or me because he never took the game seriously. "Josh, don't—"

"One other thing, Luke." Josh cradles the phone. "You got to make me a promise. No matter what happens to kick you back, you always push forward."

"I'll do my best, Josh."

"I said that's not enough!" He points at his blue county jumpsuit. "You're gonna wear an NBA jersey, not one of these. Promise me." I promise him. Mom watches us both, her eyes filled with tears.

SATURDAY EVENING
FEBRUARY 18
Tuxedo Park

The smack of the ball off the backboard sounds like a fist against a face. Scott elbows me in the side to get in position to snatch the rebound. He is older and stronger but has fewer tools. The response he gets is a harder elbow. "Don't do it again," I say.

Tony, his teammate, cackles. Kevin doesn't react other than a cold stare at Scott.

"What're you gonna do about it?" Scott's in

my face, almost. I've got five inches on him.

"He's just a kid," Kevin says. I want to correct him. I'm the only man here. I get up every morning before sunrise. I go to school during the week and work a job on the weekend. I'm responsible, and that makes me a man, not a kid. "Besides, Mark wouldn't like you hassling Li'l Mark. Right, Tony?"

Tony agrees, so Scott backs down. He fist-bumps me hard enough to break the skin.

"When you're done playing ball," Kevin says, "Mark says you should join our crew."

I could be wearing three hoodies and those words would still chill me.

"What about it?" Tony asks. They have me surrounded, boxing me in. "You gonna work at Ryan's all your life?"

Are they testing me? Teasing me? I compare the worn watchband on my wrist with the sparkling gold on Tony's. Gold jewelry hangs from his ears and around his neck. If he dips his left hand that sports two gold rings into his pocket, Tony will come up with a wad of green bills.

"No, I won't work at Ryan's all my life," I say, all serious, which just makes them laugh.

"Listen, Li'l Mark. Bet you think you'll play college or pro ball," Scott snorts. "So do half the guys who have ever passed through this court. Know how many of them made it? Probably none. You've gotta make a life. You can scrub dishes, or you can work for Mark. Help him out, and he'll help you out. He's your *family*, kid."

I bounce the ball up and down, keeping time with my heart beating fast. Scott's offering me a bite of the juicy apple and I'm feeling hungry. How much longer can I resist what seems inevitable? But if I work for Mark, I'll lose my family too. Money comes in; Mom goes out.

It was one thing to hear those words from Mr. Edwards, but it's another to hear them from Mark's friends. They don't say anything, I guess, unless Mark approves. They're his messengers.

"We'll see." I grab the ball, dribble hard, leap high, and jam it down. Birmingham is called the magic city, but I will turn the playoffs into Luke's Dunk Town and prove these guys, Grandma, Mr. Edwards, but mostly Mark, wrong. I have one direction. I move forward, not back.

FRIDAY MORNING
FEBRUARY 24
Jackson High School gym

The assembled student body roars in approval as Coach ends his pep talk by yelling, "We are going to win tonight and again on Saturday. We will be state champions!"

He had wanted players to speak, but I got out of it. Instead, I sit in my chair looking clumsy and feeling awkward, even more so when I catch a glimpse of graceful Trina up in the stands.

Once the assembly is over, everybody heads back to class. But not me. I have to see Mr. Edwards. Coach got me scholarship forms, saying, "Not *if*, Lucas, but *when* the offers come."

Outside the gym, Trina yells my name. "I hope you win tonight, Lucas!" She makes her way through the crowd to where I'm standing.

"Thanks, Trina," I say politely like Mom taught me. Trina always uses that word "hope" like Mom and Grandma. They think if they pray or hope hard enough that life will change. But it doesn't. Mom and Grandma were born poor and unless I make it, they'll die poor too. Mom's back still hurts, so she can't go to either of her jobs. Josh has no money, and she won't take Mark's money.

"Didn't you hear Coach?" I say, and I try not to smile too wide. "He says we're going to win. I know he's right. We're the best team in the state."

"You are so confident!" says the always-upbeat Trina. "I wish I could be that way."

I shrug my shoulders, which need to be

strong and broad to carry the team to a win. "I think it's not so much that I'm confident," I say. "I'm cornered. An animal never fights harder than when it is trapped. I don't want to get trapped here."

Suddenly, Trina steps forward and kisses me on the cheek. She runs away before she can see my face flush like somebody smeared my cheeks with strawberry jam. I turn around to see Nate.

"You got it all!" Nate mocks me since he knows I got nothing.

"All I got is the will to win." I tuck my chin against my chest and walk away, fast.

FRIDAY AFTERNOON
FEBRUARY 24
Jackson High School

Mr. Edwards clicks the pen almost in time with the seconds ticking on the clock on the wall. He's looking over the financial aid form he had asked me to fill out. Mom hates filling out forms and always says she's too busy, but since she's not working, she lost that excuse. He points at the phone number space on the form. It is blank. "You forgot to fill that out," he says, sounding bored.

Rather than tell him that Mom and I don't have a phone, I write in the number to Ryan's.

"And on this line." He jabs the silver pen at the line for parental income. "This should be total monthly income." He doesn't ask outright if I've filled out that line correctly, but I get that he thinks the number's too low to be right.

"I'll fix it," I say, except it's not a mistake. That's what Mom brings home, even with two jobs. I figure LeBron makes per minute more than Mom earns all year. "Anything else?"

"Just sign here to say that you're not lying on this form." He laughs. I don't know why. "Which is ironic, because if you get accepted on an athletic scholarship, they're going to lie to you, Lucas. The recruiters will tell you a bunch of stuff and none of it will turn out to be true. Trust me."

I would not trust this man with anything, especially my future. He continues, "So, if you don't get a scholarship, what do you plan to do? Did you talk to Russell about trade school like I told you?"

I shouldn't feel bad, but I do. I hide my face.

"I want to be on the court, not under a car."

He sighs. "How about your mother, siblings, other relatives? Do they have careers that interest you?" He fakes caring like an expert.

"My mom works in the hospital. Mrs. Thompson thought maybe I could do that too. Maybe study to be a doctor or something?" Edwards scratches the back of his head with fury but says nothing, which says everything. He clicks his pen to cover the big silence in his small office.

FRIDAY EVENING FEBRUARY 24
Birmingham Convention Complex
Game 4

The crowd roars as loud as a jet engine. I can only guess, having never been on a plane. For the first time, we're playing in Birmingham, so our own fans fill half the stands. Since we're up against nearby Homewood, their fans are backed by a band, making it a contest of whose side can be louder.

But that contest is nothing like the one on

the court. All game, the lead has switched back and forth. They hit a three, we hit a triple. They sink two from the line, we do the same. They're a little faster with their guards going coast-to-coast. Elijah's trying not to show it, but he's out of gas. Jeremy got into foul trouble early, so Nate took his minutes. Nate can fill the spot, but not Jeremy's shoes.

Coach calls time with ten seconds left. We're down by two. "Lucas, Paul, and Nate. I want all three of you at the top of the key. Elijah, you set close. When David inbounds, the three of you all break for your points on the line. Elijah, find Lucas. Pass it to him, and cut toward the basket. They'll think the ball's coming back to you for the tie, but we're going for the win. Lucas, the shot is yours." We bang fists and get ourselves into position to win the game.

The ball comes in. Eight seconds. The three of us break and Elijah finds me. Six seconds. It goes like Coach said, except I don't have a good shot. I duck, fake—nothing. Four seconds. Paul comes down low, but the pass isn't there. There's one play. Three seconds.

I hurl the ball in between outstretched Homewood hands. Nate gathers it and fires an off-balance jumper from a foot outside the three-point line. It hits the rim and falls straight down as the buzzer sounds. The Jackson side of the stands explodes in applause. Someone starts chanting Nate's name. Nate made the shot, but Coach knows I made the play. That's what counts.

One other person knows that: Coach's friend, the recruiter I've yet to meet. Coach told me he'd be in the stands. My guess is that he's not cheering or chanting Nate's name. The only sound, I hope, is his pen etching the name "Lucas Washington" on a letter of intent for Long Beach State.

SATURDAY MORNING
FEBRUARY 25
On the bus from Gardendale

The bass and treble spill out of the cheap headphones that this kid about my age is wearing. Every thirty seconds or so, he gets really animated, making wild gestures with both his hands. I'd like to sleep, but his noise drowns out my beach waves. I'm also too pumped up from the victory last night, from talking to Trina on the bus this morning, and for the state championship game tonight.

When the bus makes a wide turn, the two bags of groceries I got at Foodland spill on the floor. As I pick up the food, I add up in my head how much money will be left over from my next paycheck. With no money coming in except what I make, I'll have to start hitting the church pantries again.

Mr. Robbins offered to let me have the morning off to rest up for the game, but I told him no. He told me I'm dedicated. I am. Not to him or to Ryan's but to helping Mom and me get out of here someday, maybe to California. Here, no matter how bright the sun, it always seems gray.

The wide streets of the city are free of cars, except those that are so patched up that I don't know how they don't fall apart with all the potholes that the city never fixes. There are some people walking down the sidewalks, always in small groups. Nobody feels safe alone. The pitted sidewalk is filled with cigarette butts. Each block looks the same: house, vacant lot, house for sale, deserted house, and house with an overgrown lawn.

Nobody has any money here except the people taking the little bit of money the poor people have to spend. At the corner, there are a few stores, only about half of them open at this hour of the morning. Check-cashing places next to pawnshops next to the corner store selling lottery tickets. There are no decent places to eat or get fresh vegetables, but every big intersection has a church. Spirit full, but belly empty.

The guy in the headphones gets off at the stop before mine. As soon as he's off the bus, he pulls out a smoke and lights it. The smoke makes the sky grayer. He heads for a corner store with the words *beer*, *wine*, and *lottery* in neon lights. I pull the cord and gather my things. This is my stop, but no matter what, I'm not staying here. These sidewalks won't suck me down.

SATURDAY AFTERNOON
FEBRUARY 25
Lucas Washington's apartment

Mom groans in pain when I help her out of bed. She leans on me to stand and get her balance. "Luke, I'm so sorry," Mom says. Her teeth clench in pain; her eyes squint in agony.

"Mom, why don't you see a doctor?" I deflect.

Mom shakes her head. That looks like it hurts too. The back is like the point guard in basketball: everything runs through it. Bad back, bad body. "How am I gonna afford that?"

This is Mom's answer to almost any question for as long as I've asked. "I bet Mark—"

She rears her hand as if to strike me. "I'll be fine." I hate when Mom lies to me.

"You want to visit Josh today?" Another head-shake answer. "I know it means—"

"Luke, I'm sorry I failed as a mother," Mom says. "Like Josh said, it's up to you. I don't mean playing in the NBA like he said, but just doing right. Stay in school and stay out of trouble. Can you do that for me? Lord, I don't ask for much and I don't expect anything. Can you?"

I hug Mom, which I bet hurts, but it's the only response I've got. I help her walk toward the kitchen, not that there's much of anything to eat. "I'd do anything for you. You know that?"

Mom starts to cry—silent tears because loud sobs would hurt too much. "I know."

"You know why?" I ask, but don't give her a chance to answer. "It is not just because you're my mom, but because of everything you did for me and for Josh and Mark. You passed it forward. You helped me up and supported me when I needed it. It is my turn."

Mom and I walk together slowly toward the kitchen. We reach the table and she sits.

"You want some coffee?" All that's left are the grounds of my coffee. She waves it off.

"All I want is for you to win that championship. I'll pray for you." I don't ask how God decides between the prayers of Mom and those of the mom of the Carver team's forward.

"If I had money, I'd bet on it," I say with the pride of someone who knows his future.

SATURDAY EVENING FEBRUARY 25

Birmingham Convention Complex
Game 5

I don't know what an earthquake sounds
like, but this has to be close. With Carver
and Jackson fans stomping the old wood
bleachers, the floor seems to be shaking—and
I'm shaking as I finally stop to look up at the
scoreboard. We're up sixty-six to sixty-three
with a minute left.

"Lucas, you okay?" Coach asks. "You're

trying too hard and trying to do too much."

I nod my sweaty head in agreement. I've gotten points, but few assists or boards. Almost every time I get the ball, I shoot it. I'm good, but even hitting fifty from the floor and a hundred from the line isn't what the team needs. I know that. I glance at the stands and wonder what the pack of college recruiters and maybe—*dream, baby, dream!*—somebody from the Grizzlies wants me to do.

"Slow down, Luke," Elijah reminds me. Coach and the other starters agree.

I don't tell them I've only got one speed: full-force gale like a hurricane. "I know. I know."

I head back onto the court. I see Trina in the stands. No Mom or Mark, but it is a big crowd, so I tell myself that I might just be missing them. But then I remind myself to get rid of the fantasy that Mark's going to leave his life of crime and Mom's going to welcome him back into the family.

I set up down low. Elijah dribbles and I cut up. He passes me the ball. I see daylight, just a sliver in the gray between the defender and the baseline. They double-team me. It creates nothing but blue sky for Paul. I bounce it toward him. Two. And a foul. Make it three.

As the seconds tick down and we hold onto our thin lead, Coach, who is normally smart, yells out the stupidest thing: "Let's think out there!" It feels like he's yelling only at me.

Doesn't he know that I play at this level on pure instinct? Since I first touched a ball at maybe age three to the first time I saw Mark play. From the first time I shot a jumper to the first time I stuffed the ball. From then until now, it has all led to this moment. This time and place.

Their forward gets the ball, fakes a pass, and tries a baseline jumper. I time it perfectly and smash the ball back in his face. Life's done that to me. It is about time that I paid it back.

SUNDAY MORNING
FEBRUARY 26
Ryan's Steak Buffet

The bing-bing of the bus cord wakes me up. I look over at Trina. She's the one who pulled it. I was so tired from staying up all night celebrating with the team that I barely made it out of bed. "You saved me," I tell her. She smiles in return. That saves me a little bit too.

"So are you going to work more now that the season is over?" she asks. She's getting off in front of Ryan's too. Wal-Mart is at least two stops away. I nod my sleepy head.

"We can catch the bus right in front of school." I like the word "we" from her lips. "I mean, that is, if you're staying in school now that the season is over. I hope you do, Lucas."

"I have to graduate." I then tell her about Coach saying that his California friend will offer me an athletic scholarship. I point at my CD player. "Maybe I'll hear the beach for real."

She talks about going to Jefferson State Community College. She chats the entire walk to the Ryan's employee door. "I gotta go," I say. Then I lean over to kiss her. Trina doesn't back up; she pushes forward. The door opens and Mr. Robbins stands there gawking. I feel embarrassed.

I walk inside. Mr. Robbins invites Trina to join us. Where I normally dump my bus tray is a big cake. Written on it is "Congratulations, Lucas!" Nobody's *ever* done this for me before.

"You made the front page." Mr. Robbins holds up the local newspaper. Not just the sports section, but the first section of the whole paper. It is a photo of my blocked shot in the closing seconds.

I take the paper in my hands. It is like I'm holding a pile of bills, investing in my future.

"We're proud of you," Mr. Robbins says—like, I imagine, a dad might proclaim. People applaud. They're coworkers, but at this minute, it almost feels like they're family. Trina hangs on my arm, which makes me feel strong and safe. I gaze at the photo. Up front there's me looking so tough, but I look at the faces in the background. I can't make any of them out, so it is easy to pretend that one of them is Mark feeling proud of me too.

SUNDAY AFTERNOON
FEBRUARY 26
Grandma Washington's house

The doorbell chimes at Grandma's house. It takes a little time for her to get to the door, but once she does, it takes no time for her to shoot a look of scorn since I'm not alone. Not with Mom, but with Trina. Nor am I empty-handed. I march into her house and place the tournament MVP trophy on her table.

"Get that off my table." Grandma shuts— actually, slams—the door behind us.

I leave the trophy on the table. I help Trina with her coat. I take our coats, which are covered with rare Alabama snowflakes, to the coat rack by the front door, where Grandma stands.

"At the start of the season, everybody said we had a snowball's chance in hell," I tell Trina, since Grandma's not talking to me. All Grandma's energy goes into that glare. "But here we are."

"Take that off *my* table." Grandma repeats. She re-opens the door, her message clear.

"No." As I say the word, I think about my family and our lives. What if Mom and those guys would've said "no" and not had two kids before they were eighteen? What if Josh would've said "no" to the guys selling him drugs? What if Mark would've said "no" to the guys getting him to deal? One tiny word would've changed one life big-time. Mine.

"I will not tell you again." The tone tells me what we both already know. This isn't about the trophy but her lack of faith in me. I proved her wrong, and Grandma is always right.

"Lucas, please, show some respect," Trina whispers.

"I am, for myself," I answer. Grandma chatters about praying to the Lord for strength.

"Do it for me, please." Another Trina whisper. I return to the table and remove the trophy. I cradle it in my lap like I'll do with my son or daughter when I teach them to say "no."

Grandma closes the door. She walks to the table and then sits and starts to pray, again.

I hang my head and mumble the words that Grandma says and Trina repeats. Grandma believes that praying hard is the path to an easier life. I proved that *playing* hard is my way forward.

SUNDAY EVENING
FEBRUARY 26
Tuxedo Park

The dented snow shovel scrapes against the pavement. We clear it to get a game going, but I don't know if we'll play since all Mark's friends seem like they'd rather put me down than throw shots up.

"Mr. Cock of the Walk," Scott says. He puts his hands under his shoulders and parades around the court pretending to be a rooster. I keep shoveling. Mark's friends keep laughing.

Tony pitches in, kicking snow with his big, clumsy feet. "Mr. MVP. Mr. Front Page!"

"I'm going to college," I say to shut them up. It just makes it worse. They rag on me harder, but I continue, "I don't even know which one. Coach says recruiters are going to be all over me."

By the time the court's uncovered, they've run out of insults. Once we start to play, Tony and Scott hack with machete hands every time I touch the tingly cold basketball.

"Knock it off," I tell Tony. "That's a foul."

"Toughen up, college boy" is his first response. Another hack is his second. I hurl the ball to the pavement and walk away. "Before you know it, you're going to be back here, Li'l Mark."

I stop and realize *that's* what this is all about. I'm moving forward. They're standing still. I don't turn around as I listen to Tony and Scott call me out, until Kevin shuts them down.

"Li'l Mark!" Kevin runs and catches up with me. "Mark wants you to know something."

I turn around. The air's so icy I can see my breath. Even it looks gray. "What?" I snap.

"He wanted me to tell you that he's proud of you." Kevin puts out his fist for a bump.

I put my hands in my pockets. I think about Mom on the bus in the morning and Mark in his Mustang, out partying all night. I think how I wanted to be Mark from the first time I saw him dunk. He was my hero, but I will not follow his path. "Can you tell him something for me?" I ask.

"What?" Kevin smiles. He must not notice that my voice is colder than this snow.

Another flash at Mom's life compared to Mark's. "Tell him that I'm *not* proud of him."

TUESDAY MORNING
FEBRUARY 28
Jackson High School

The hard slap of a hand on my baggy new
Long Beach State T-shirt, courtesy of Coach's
recruiter friend, echoes in the small science
lab. "Congrats, Lucas," Joshua says. He's not
the first one. For the past two days, that's all
I've heard, sometimes from people I barely
know giving me hand slaps, high fives, and
hosannas for winning state, getting named
MVP, and the story in the paper. They're

giving me props for reaching the first rung of the ladder out of here.

I thank him. I'm going to have to get used to speaking to people I don't know before I start talking to recruiters. Coach told me yesterday that I can use his phone and office to talk to them, but he wants to be there too.

"Yes, congratulations, Elijah and Lucas. You've made everyone in this school very proud," Mrs. Thompson says. She points at both of us and then claps. Everybody else joins in.

"But now our focus must return to the classroom," she starts. I take notes, writing down every word she says like it's gospel. I don't stop until the bell rings. She stops me as I exit.

"Did I do something wrong?" I ask her. Mrs. Thompson points to the empty chair by her desk. I sit.

"I understand from Mr. Unser that you might go to college. I'm proud of you, Lucas." I blush in every shade of red on the spectrum. "What will you study? Pre-med? Chemistry?"

Students for the next class start to file in, picking up their lab notebooks. I'm silent as I watch them copying Mrs. Thompson's notes on the chalkboard.

"I will study education," I finally say. "I want to be a science teacher like you."

She laughs kindly. "Lucas, that's nice, but you should aim big. You should—"

I turn and look at the students who come to class every day with odds against them, as much as me, maybe more so. Beaten down by economics, but raised up by education. "I am."

"Lucas, that's very nice." She's all flustered. "But maybe you should consider something other than teaching—"

"I'd agree with you, Mrs. Thompson," I say and then smile. "But then we'd both be wrong."

TUESDAY AFTERNOON
FEBRUARY 28
Jackson High School cafeteria

That afternoon, I skip my appointment with
Mr. Edwards, where he would have just told
me all the same things. Instead, I use my time
smartly. Mr. Edwards can't argue with that.

I see Russell Walker banging two metal
spoons against the cafeteria table, playing
drums along with whatever music pours
through the leaky headphones barely hanging
on his pierced ears.

I walk up to Russell and tap him on the shoulder. He puts down the spoons. He sits on the table next to his tray without a speck of food on it, holding a CD player more busted-up than mine.

"Hey, congratulations on your championship," Russell says. "I got one more chance. But even if we do win, I doubt I'll be getting one of those MVP trophies." I know from sports banquets that Russell plays football, wrestles, and catches in baseball. He's built like a fireplug.

"Don't say that," I tell him. He kicks the empty chair toward me so I can sit.

"Hey, easy for you. You got on the front page of the paper. You'll go to college and—"

"Mr. Edwards said you're going to trade school, so it seems like you have a plan."

Russell laughs. "Big difference between college and A+ Auto Mechanics school."

"Different roads maybe, but both a path out of here." I stare at the empty cafeteria chairs around us. In my head, I start listing the names of all the people I knew who used to fill them. Some dropped out, some got kicked out. Some are behind bars, some are buried under the ground. "Any honest path will do."

"Maybe," he says. Not yes, or no, but maybe. A shade of gray. It fits this place. Then we start talking, and I'm surprised by how much we have in common. We chat until the bell rings. "I gotta go."

"Me too." I race not toward the door but to the lunch line. I grab handfuls of fresh fruit and take them to checkout. The checkout lady motions for the MVP to pass by without paying.

"Thanks." I bite into the green apple easily, thinking how hard it's been for me to resist the green that Mark offers. That's an apple filled with nothing but worms.

TUESDAY EVENING
FEBRUARY 28
Lucas Washington's apartment

Mom's going to try to go back to work at the nursing home. "I hurt too bad to lift people at the hospital," Mom says.

I finish off the dinner of salty beans and rice with a side of Dollar Tree canned veggies. "Is there anything I can do?" I ask. I ask her every day and "no" is always her answer. Until now.

"You can sit with me for a while." That is

odd, because normally after dinner, I get a game until my curfew to study, and Mom reads library books. Although the past two days, the only physical activity I've gotten after school is kissing Trina. "I feel nervous about going back to work."

This somehow leads to her telling stories about growing up in Birmingham. "I never got out, like Rachel. I made some bad choices. Like Josh did. Like Mark does. But not you, Lucas."

"I'm doing my best for both of us. I just hope I don't get hurt playing ball, like Mark."

Mom's eyes go glassy. Her jaw drops open. "I know that's what we told you, but that's not it. You should know. He got kicked off that team for selling drugs."

I feel like I've been punched. He was my hero for a long time, even if he hasn't been recently. "But his ankle?"

"He broke that running from the cops," Mom says. "We lied to you, Lucas. I knew how much you respected and admired him. I didn't want to shatter that when you were young."

"I know what he is now." Why am I shocked he was that way back in the day? But I am.

"And that's all that matters," Mom says. "Don't look back. Look forward."

Mom and me talk until it's time for bed, mostly about my possible future. I don't talk about the NBA or getting drafted, just about going to college and doing well there. Small dreams.

As she heads off for bed, Mom calls out, "Mark didn't break just his ankle." Mom's crying now. I head back toward her, but she waves me away. "He broke his life—and my heart."

She turns off the light. I lie on the sofa and close my eyes. My ears await the alarm clock buzzer.

Check out all the titles in the

bOUNCE

Collection

AT THE
CENTER

PASS IT
FORWARD

ON
GUARD

TO THE
POINT

WELCOME TO the DOJO

LEARN TO FIGHT,
LEARN TO LIVE,
AND LEARN
TO FIGHT
FOR YOUR
LIFE.

BODY SHOT
PATRICK JONES

SIDE CONTROL
PATRICK JONES

HEAD KICK
PATRICK JONES

TRIANGLE CHOKE
PATRICK JONES

ABOUT THE AUTHOR

Patrick Jones is a former librarian for teenagers. He received lifetime achievement awards from the American Library Association and the Catholic Library Association in 2006. Jones has authored several titles for the following Darby Creek series: Turbocharged (2013); Opportunity (2013); The Dojo (2013), which won the YALSA Quick Picks for Reluctant Young Adult Readers award; The Red Zone (2014); The Alternative (2014); Bareknuckle (2014); and Locked Out (2015). He also authored *The Main Event: The Moves and Muscle of Pro Wrestling* (2013), which was placed on the Chicago Public Library's Best of the Best Books list. While Patrick lives in Minneapolis, he still considers Flint, Michigan, his home. He can be found on the web at www.connectingya.com.